This book belongs to

_____

Dedicated to my cousin John Francis Lawler IV and my nephew Greyson Dale Legault. Your time with us was short, but your influence everlasting. You will always be loved, forever be missed, and never forgotten.

For more information or to order a copy visit:

http://www.adoodlebugbook.com/hooray_for_prek

A DoodleBug Book

www.adoodlebugbook.com

Hooray for Pre-K

Written by Cathleen D. Mayo
Illustrated by Michael Conley

Morning has come,
and the day is finally here.
This is my first time in pre-k,
and it is going to be a great year.

I hurry out of bed,
and throw my big boy clothes on.
The time is going to fly right by,
and soon I will be gone.

I am heading off to pre-k,
for a day filled with excitement and new friends.
I can't wait to get to my new classroom,
where the fun never ends.

I have finally arrived,
and I am putting my backpack away.
There is my name tag,
it reads "Johnny, We Welcome You To Pre K."

I look all around,
and see smiling friendly faces everywhere.
All the school supplies, toys and cubbies,
so much cool new stuff we all get to share.

It's hard to choose which direction I should go.
Calendar to the left and sensory to the right.
I want to see everything there is to see,
and play with all of it I just might.

My teachers are so much fun,
playing games and reading books aloud.
It's hard to not feel right at home here
in this brand new and exciting crowd.

Even the food is delicious...
chicken tenders, beans and fruit.
I gobble it all right up,
knowing for sure the beans will make me toot.

Now to use the potty,
and wash my hands again.
I have done it so much already.
How many times? I bet at least ten.

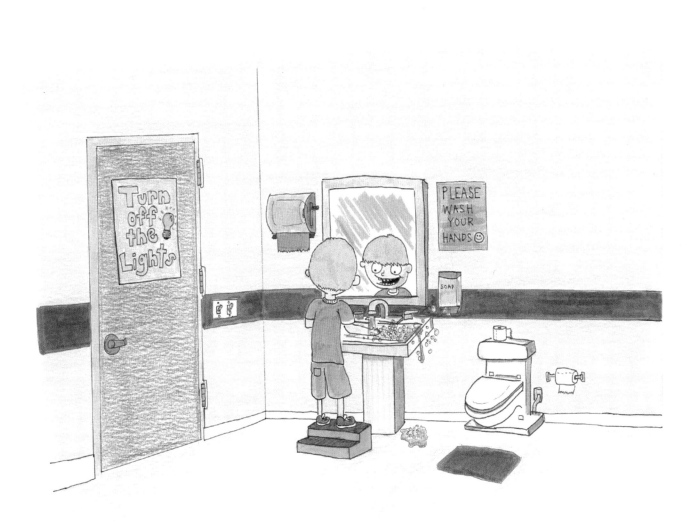

The lights go out.
and the mats are laid down.
It's time to rest my tired body,
the room doesn't make a sound.

Now I am up,
it's time for me to head home.
I think of all the new friends I've made,
and how I will never be alone.

What a day!
I Love Pre-K!

The End

Made in the USA
Monee, IL
23 August 2022

12241621R00019